A, B, Sea

A Deep-Sea Symphony

Dianna Bonder

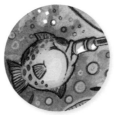

WALRUS

The audience assembles; the auditorium trembles;
the ambient light fades away.
As angelfish wait, they anticipate;
the orchestra then starts to play.

Beginning in B, then C, D and E,
the bagpipes belt out a tune.
They bellow and bleep, they boom and they beep
while a blowfish blows its bassoon.

Continuing on, the clarinets' song;

their crystal-clear notes charm the crowd.

Then cymbals go *crack!* And clamshells go *clack!*

And the catfishes' cellos chirr loud.

Then dogfish keep beat, on drums with their feet,
dramatic, decisive, demanding.
The dolphins dive in and dizzily spin.
The dazzled crowd deems it outstanding!

Now enter the eels' electrical squeals,
lighting the depths of the ocean.
Euphoniums squeak and eerily shriek;
their echoes evoke such emotion.

The flounder fish floats with four perfect notes,
fingering the keys on the flute.
Then flotsam floats free, footloose in the sea
with F notes hot in pursuit.

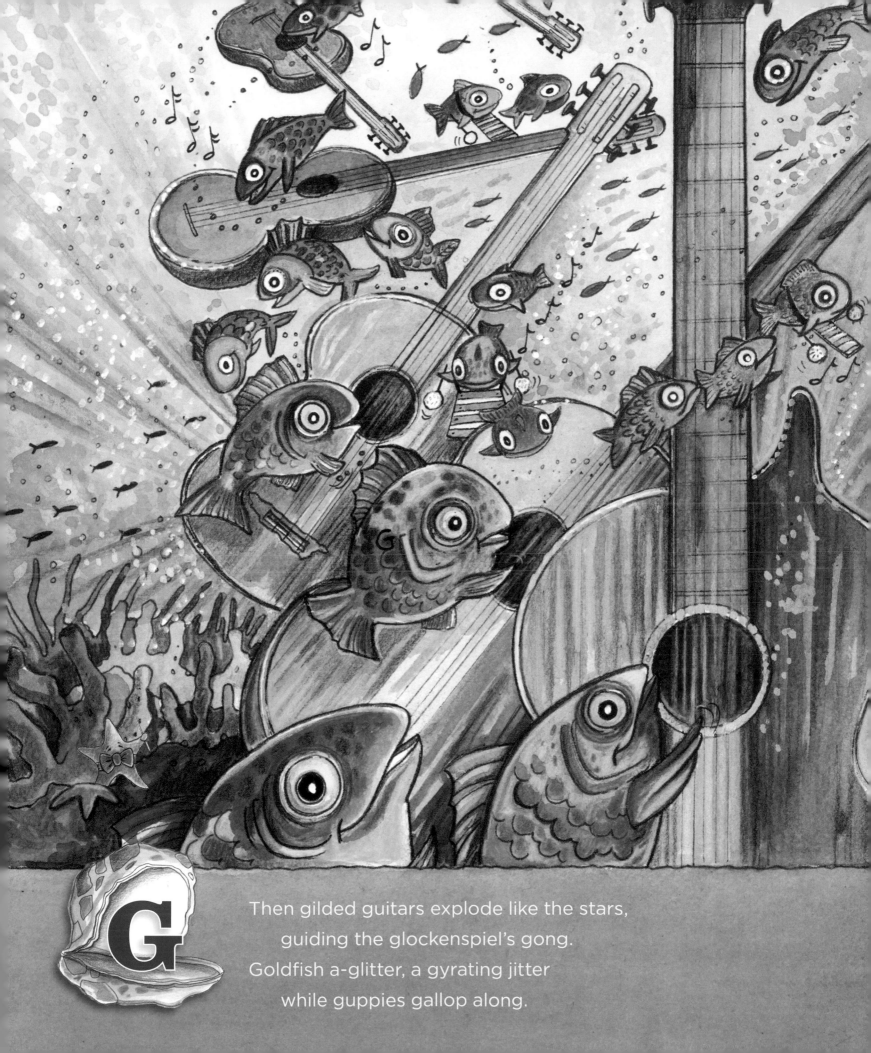

Then gilded guitars explode like the stars,
guiding the glockenspiel's gong.
Goldfish a-glitter, a gyrating jitter
while guppies gallop along.

Hear hammerhead sharks play humpback-whale harps.

Harmoniums heave *one, two, three*.

Then halibut fins play halibut hymns

as the horns hypnotize the sea.

Indelible ink! From where, do you think?
Octopuses inking the show!
Their insides are leaking—black and blue streaking—
the instruments covered. *Oh no!*

J Jellyfish jump and joyfully bump
through jade-coloured waters so deep.
They jet through the ink and slowly they sink
into a jellyfish sleep.

The khaki-green kelp then offer their help
to clean up the maestro's baton.
With king crabs and krill, they mop up the spill.
Hooray! The show can go on!

Lime-coloured limpets lick up the missed bits
as languishing lobsters recline.
In lava-red suits they pick up their lutes
then lazily roll into line.

The mandolins move the musical groove
through melon-shaped moon snails at night.
Then marlins at play move every which way
as mussels march into the light.

The noise is profound, a noteworthy sound.

But look! The narwhals are here.

They round up the notes in nautilus boats

and soon all the sounds disappear.

The ocean swells churn and notes soon return;
the orchestra works through the score.
The oboe's odd song from the octopus strong,
unveils the oysters on shore.

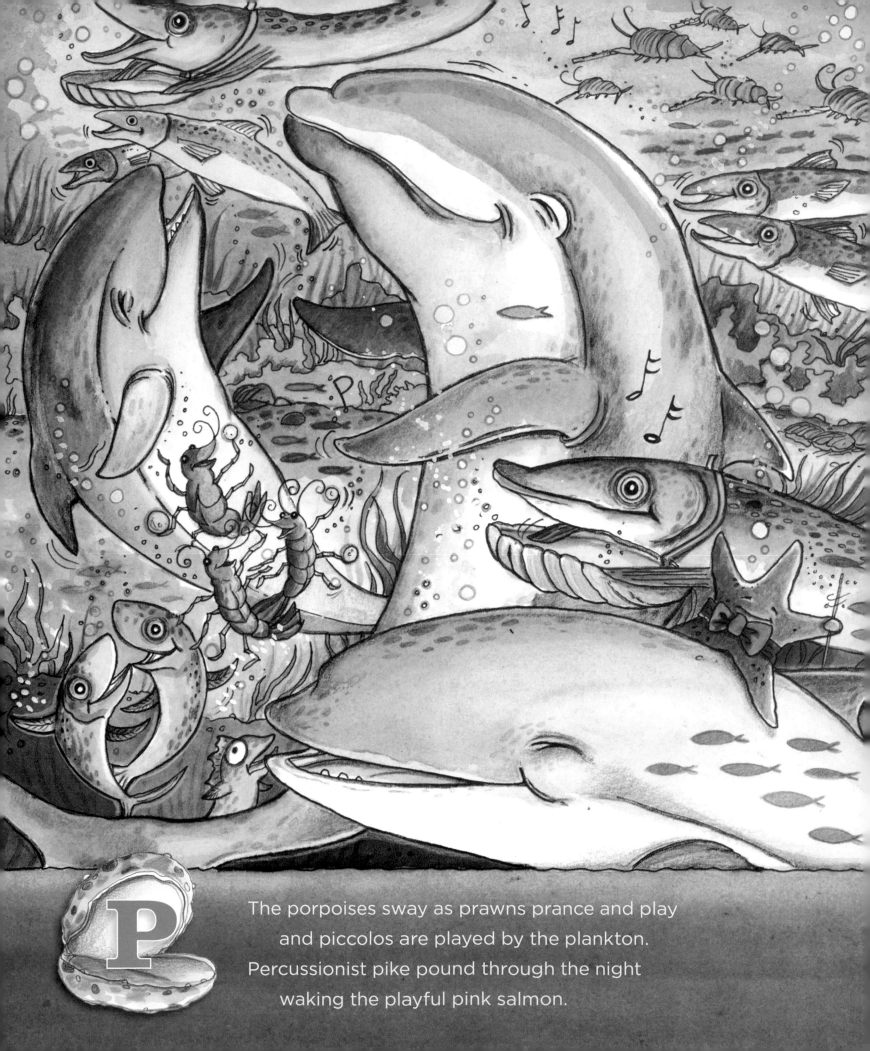

The porpoises sway as prawns prance and play
and piccolos are played by the plankton.
Percussionist pike pound through the night
waking the playful pink salmon.

Then quick as can be, the rambunctious sea
is quelled by the quahogs' soft hum.
The ocean's fine brine like quicksand keeps time
till each quiet quahog is done.

Radiant rays roll over waves;
  rhythmic recorders rejoice.
Rollicking rockfish join in the chorus,
  using their rockfishy voice.

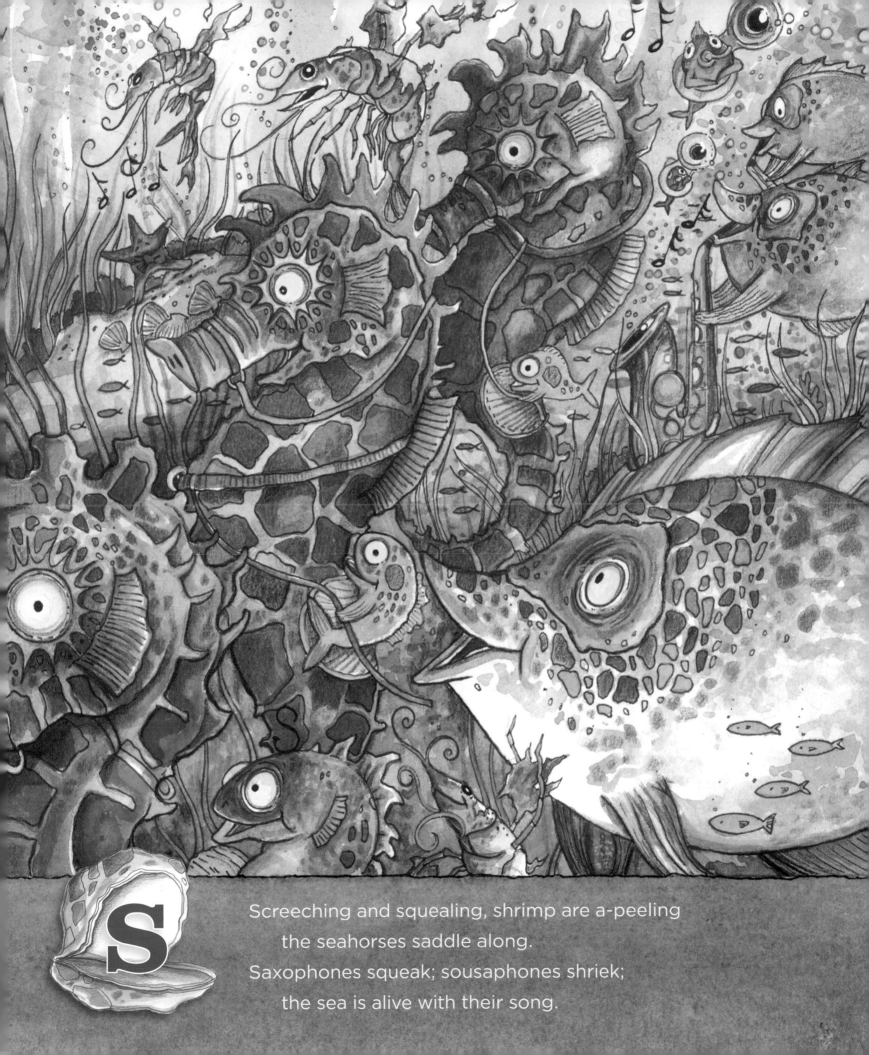

Screeching and squealing, shrimp are a-peeling
the seahorses saddle along.
Saxophones squeak; sousaphones shriek;
the sea is alive with their song.

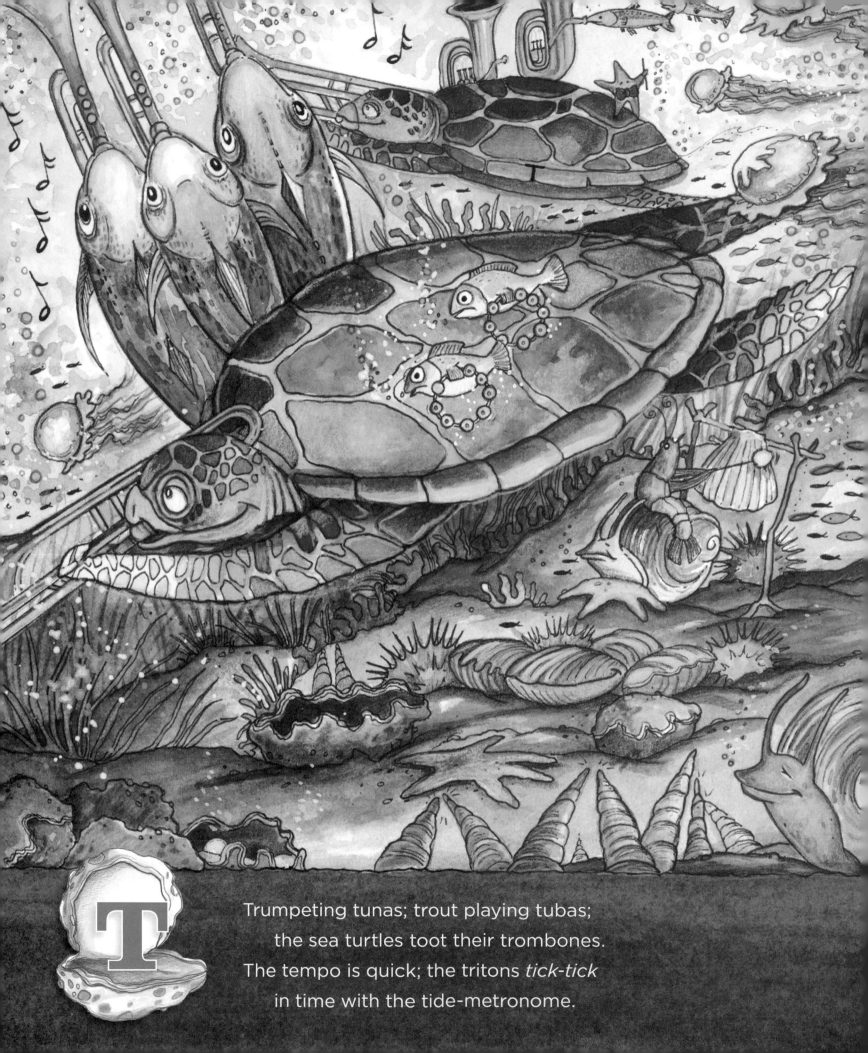

Trumpeting tunas; trout playing tubas;
the sea turtles toot their trombones.
The tempo is quick; the tritons *tick-tick*
in time with the tide-metronome.

Then urchins of green and ultramarine
bob up-down and up-down and up.
Untimely and slow, they upset the show
until the maestro yells, "Stop!"

Then raising his hands, he voices commands,
inviting the veenas to play.
So velvety smooth, they weave a new groove
as violins vanish away.

The welcoming whales *whick-whack* their tails
while whistling whelks wash in slow.
The woodwinds blow through, with little to do;
it's almost the end of the show!

Explosive! Exciting! The show is enlightening!
Exceeding our high expectations!
The xylophones tap! The x-ray eels zap!
The crowd gives a standing ovation.

"Yippee" and "Yay," the listeners all say.

"What a thrill!" "What a sound!" "What a night!"

Then closing the show, the yellow jacks throw

confetti with youthful delight.

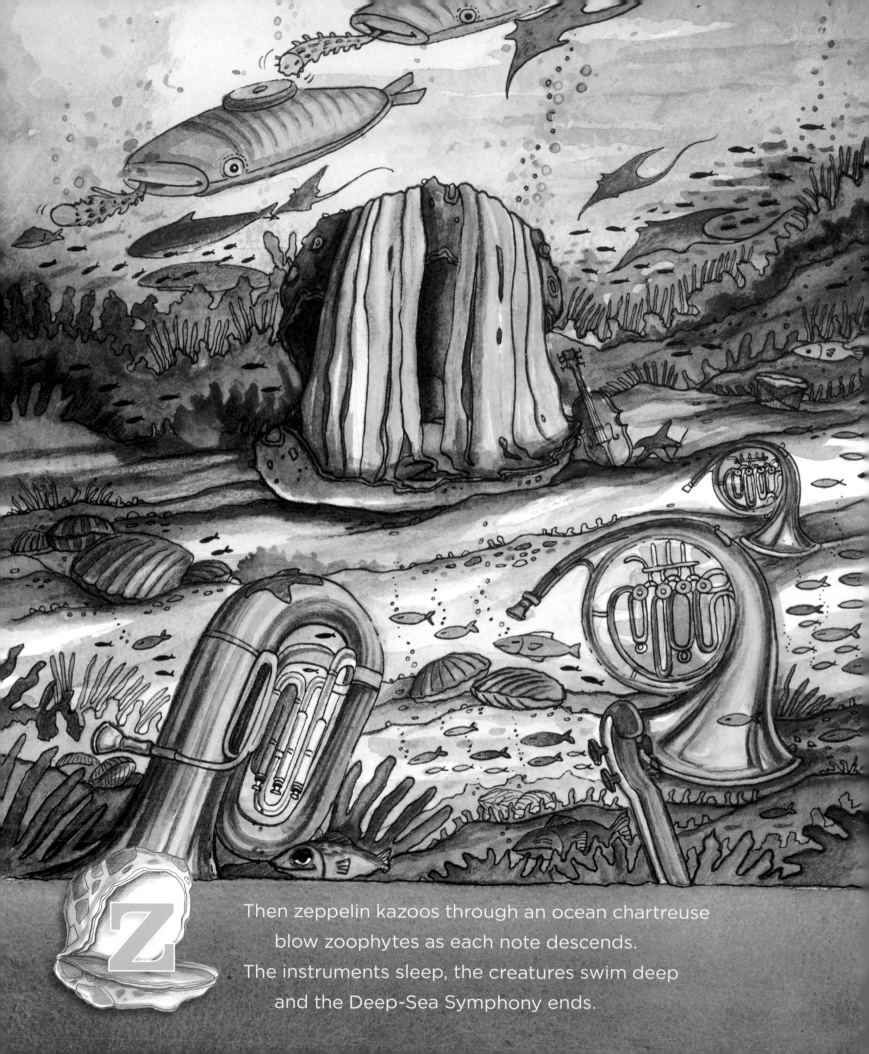

Then zeppelin kazoos through an ocean chartreuse
blow zoophytes as each note descends.
The instruments sleep, the creatures swim deep
and the Deep-Sea Symphony ends.

Did you find all the hidden objects? Turn the page to see.

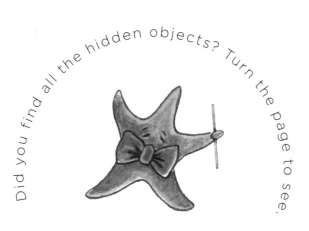

Find the hidden letter and the starfish maestro on each page.

What else can you find?

Aa

CAN YOU FIND?—angelfish, audience, auditorium (and the orchestra)
HIDDEN LETTER—in the marking on the back of the angelfish at the bottom right
STARFISH MAESTRO—standing on the large pearl in the centre

Bb

CAN YOU FIND?—bagpipes, bassoon, blowfish
HIDDEN LETTER—on the blowfish at the top left
STARFISH MAESTRO—in the auditorium toward the top right

Cc

CAN YOU FIND?—catfish, cellos, clamshells, clarinets, crab, cymbals
HIDDEN LETTER—in the clamshell at the right edge
STARFISH MAESTRO—in the clamshell at the right edge

Dd

CAN YOU FIND?—dogfish, dolphins, drums
HIDDEN LETTER—on the "foot" of the second dogfish from the top
STARFISH MAESTRO—on the back of the dolphin at the to p-right corner

Ee

CAN YOU FIND?—eels, euphoniums
HIDDEN LETTER—on the euphonium at the top right
STARFISH MAESTRO—in the bottom-right corner

Ff

CAN YOU FIND?—flotsam, flounder fish, flutes
HIDDEN LETTER—in the top fin of the flounder fish
STARFISH MAESTRO—on the flotsam at the top right

Gg

CAN YOU FIND?—glockenspiels, goldfish, guitars, guppies
HIDDEN LETTER—on the big guppy near the centre
STARFISH MAESTRO—in the coral at the bottom left

Hh

CAN YOU FIND?—halibut, hammerhead sharks, harmonicas, harmoniums, horns, humpback-whale harps
HIDDEN LETTER—in the strings of the humpback-whale harp at the top right
STARFISH MAESTRO—on the tail of the hammerhead shark in the centre

Ii

CAN YOU FIND?—ink (and octopuses), instruments
HIDDEN LETTER—to the left of the ink splash on the tuba at the bottom edge
STARFISH MAESTRO—on the back of the fish at the top-left corner

Jj

CAN YOU FIND?—jellyfish
HIDDEN LETTER—on the fin of the fish at the bottom right
STARFISH MAESTRO—on the sand toward the bottom right

Kk

CAN YOU FIND?—kelp (and a baton), king crabs, krill
HIDDEN LETTER—in the sand under the large king crab
STARFISH MAESTRO—at the top-right corner

Ll

CAN YOU FIND?—limpets, lionfish, lobsters, lutes
HIDDEN LETTER—on the tail of the lobster at the top left
STARFISH MAESTRO—on the sand near the top-left edge

Mm

CAN YOU FIND?—mandolins, marlins, moon snails, mussels
HIDDEN LETTER—on the shell of the moon snail at the centre bottom
STARFISH MAESTRO—on the marlin at the top left

Nn

CAN YOU FIND?—narwhals, nautiluses (and musical notes)
HIDDEN LETTER—on the shell pattern of the nautilus toward the centre right
STARFISH MAESTRO—at the bottom-right edge

Oo

CAN YOU FIND?—oboe, octopus, opah, orchestra, oysters
HIDDEN LETTER—in the bubbles under the oboe
STARFISH MAESTRO—at the bottom-left corner

Pp

CAN YOU FIND?—piccolos, pike (and salmon), plankton, porpoises, prawns
HIDDEN LETTER—on the sand in the centre
STARFISH MAESTRO—on the back of the porpoise at the bottom right

Qq

CAN YOU FIND?—quahogs
HIDDEN LETTER—on the quahog at the bottom-right corner
STARFISH MAESTRO—among the quahogs in the centre

Rr

CAN YOU FIND?—rattles, rays, recorders, rockfish
HIDDEN LETTER—near the gill of the rockfish at the bottom-right corner
STARFISH MAESTRO—on the ray in the top centre

Ss

CAN YOU FIND?—saddles, saxophones, scallops, seahorses, shrimp, sousaphones
HIDDEN LETTER—on the tail of the large red seahorse
STARFISH MAESTRO—in the sand near the top left corner

Tt

CAN YOU FIND?—sea turtles, tambourines, triton shells, trombones, trout, trumpets, tubas, tunas
HIDDEN LETTER—on the shell of the smaller sea turtle
STARFISH MAESTRO—on the back of the smaller sea turtle

Uu

CAN YOU FIND?—urchins
HIDDEN LETTER—at the bottom-left corner
STARFISH MAESTRO—at the centre right

Vv

CAN YOU FIND?—veenas, violins
HIDDEN LETTER—on the gourd of the middle veena near the top right
STARFISH MAESTRO—front and centre!

Ww

CAN YOU FIND?—whales, whelks, woodwind instruments
HIDDEN LETTER—in the waves at the centre-top edge
STARFISH MAESTRO—on the big whale in the centre

Xx

CAN YOU FIND?—x-ray eels, xylophones
HIDDEN LETTER—the openings of the bells on the necklaces of the x-ray eels
STARFISH MAESTRO—in the seaweed at the centre-left edge

Yy

CAN YOU FIND?—yellow jacks (and confetti)
HIDDEN LETTER—in the seaweed below the two big fish shaking fins in the centre
STARFISH MAESTRO—on the sand near the top-right corner

Zz

CAN YOU FIND?—(instruments), zeppelin kazoos, zoophytes
HIDDEN LETTER—in the auditorium underneath the curtains
STARFISH MAESTRO—in the sand to the right of the auditorium

To my little mermaids, Ekko and Nico.
And to the Woodcock Fund for their support.

Text and illustrations copyright © 2013 by Dianna Bonder
Walrus Books, an imprint of Whitecap Books

Edited by: Paula Ayer, Theresa Best and Taryn Boyd
Designed by: Andrew Bagatella and Michelle Furbacher

Printed in Canada

Library and Archives Canada Cataloguing in Publication

Bonder, Dianna, 1970-
     A, B, sea : a deep-sea symphony / Dianna Bonder.

ISBN 978-1-77050-043-3

1. English language--Alphabet--Juvenile literature. 2. Alphabet books.
3. Ocean--Juvenile literature. I. Title.

PE1155.B658 2012   J421'.1   C2011-908324-8

The publisher acknowledges the financial support of the Canada Council
for the Arts, the British Columbia Arts Council, and the Government
of Canada through the Canada Book Fund (CBF). Whitecap Books also
acknowledges the financial support of the Province of British Columbia
through the Book Publishing Tax Credit.

13 14 15 16 17   5 4 3 2 1

 ENVIRONMENTAL BENEFITS STATEMENT

Whitecap Books Ltd saved the following resources
by printing the pages of this book on chlorine free
paper made with 10% post-consumer waste.

TREES	WATER	ENERGY	SOLID WASTE	GREENHOUSE GASES
1	404	1	27	75
FULLY GROWN	GALLONS	MILLION BTUs	POUNDS	POUNDS

 Environmental impact estimates were made using the Environmental Paper Network
Paper Calculator 3.2. For more information visit www.papercalculator.org.